Little Sister for Sale

by Morse Hamilton

illustrated by Gioia Fiammenghi

25¢

COBBLEHILL BOOKS
Dutton   New York

Library of Congress Cataloging-in-Publication Data
Hamilton, Morse.
    Little sister for sale / by Morse Hamilton : illustrated by Gioia Fiammenghi.   p.   cm.
    Summary: Kate thinks that the antics of her little sister, Abby, are unbearable and sets
about to find another home for her but soon realizes that in spite of all she needs her.
    ISBN 0-525-65078-4
    [1. Sisters—Fiction.]   I. Fiammenghi, Gioia, ill.   II. Title.   PZ7.H18265Li   1992
[E]—dc20   91-8139   CIP   AC

Published in the United States by
Cobblehill Books,
an affiliate of Dutton Children's Books,
a division of Penguin Books USA Inc.,
375 Hudson Street, New York, NY 10014

Designed by Mina Greenstein
Printed in Hong Kong
First Edition   10 9 8 7 6 5 4 3 2 1

For Grandma Rose

—M.H.

To Laura, with love

—G.F.

"What happened to Phoebe's hair?" Kate cried, cradling her doll in her arms. "Who chopped her pigtail in half?"

Nobody answered.

Phoebe used to have *two* shiny golden braids. Kate stamped up the basement steps.

"ABBY!" she shouted. "Where are you?"

Abby wasn't in the kitchen. On the table was a dish of strawberries, though. Somebody had bitten off the good half of every one. Only the parts with the stems were left.

"ABBY!" Kate wailed. "We were supposed to share those."

There was a trail of pink sugar on the floor.

Abby wasn't under her bed, either. That's where she
hid sometimes. But Kate's favorite dinosaur book was.
Somebody had scribbled with a different color crayon
on every page. Somebody had drawn a smiley face on
Tyrannosaurus rex.

Kate scrambled out from under the bed.

"Where Are You, Abigail Wilkins Hamilton?" she growled.

The water was running in the bathroom sink.

"Oh, sick!" said Kate, wrinkling her nose. She held her
toothbrush with two fingers. It was all wet.

"You brushed your teeth with *my* toothbrush! Now it's got
your germs on it!"

"Maybe it fell in the toilet," said a small voice from the
clothes hamper.

Kate lifted the lid of the hamper.

Abby stood up. "Boo!" she cried, climbing out. "Hi, Kate. Did I scare you?"

"Abby," Kate said, "you've been a Very Bad Girl. Look what you did to poor Phoebe."

Abby looked at Phoebe. She pushed out her lips.

"Sor-ry," she said in a singsong voice. "I was giving her a haircut."

"You're not sorry," Kate said. "You're smiling. You're making your pig snout!"

Kate grabbed her arm. "Ooh!" she said through clenched teeth, "you're such a brat!"

Abby whined, "Stop it, Kate. You're hurting me." She cried, "I'm TELLING!"

At those dreaded words,
Kate's anger leaped like a lion.
She pulled her little sister down
the front stairs and out into
the backyard.

In the garage, she started rummaging through the pile of junk.

Abby squatted on the cement floor to watch. "You want to play something, Kate?" she said.

But Kate didn't answer. She yanked out the lemonade stand from last summer and started pounding it with a hammer. Whack, whack. The boards were shaking. Then she crossed out the word LEMONADE.

Kate and Abigail were in the front yard. Kate was sitting where you sit if you are selling something. Abby was up where the lemonade goes. The sign said, LITTLE SISTER FOR SALE.

"I won't use your toothbrush Ever Again," Abby was saying. "I promise. I wanted to see what it tasted like."

Kate didn't say anything. She was looking up the street for customers.

Chad from down the street zoomed by on his bike that was decorated with monsters.

"Hey, Kate," he called out. "What are you doing? Can I play, too?"

"You want to buy my little sister?" Kate called after him. "She's for sale."

Chad circled back and coasted to a stop. "You can't sell your little sister," he said. "It's against the law."

Kate made her big sister sound: ptsk!

"Your mom and dad are going to be mad," Chad said. "They like her."

Kate turned her face the other way. What *was* she going to tell her mom and dad? That Abby ran away? That a monster from space scooped her up? What little sister?

Chad started riding his bike around in circles. He said, "What if a space monster wants to buy her?"

Abby swallowed a mouthful of air. She put her face close to Kate's. Her eyes were very round.

"Don't be silly," Kate said, turning up her nose. "I would only sell my sister to somebody nice."

Chad was pedaling away as fast as he could. Over his shoulder he called out, "Yeah, well, guess what? Nobody's going to buy her. She can't even read!"

Kate stuck her tongue out at him. Abby quickly slid her hand into her big sister's and stuck her tongue out, too. "I won't draw pretty pictures in your dinosaur book ever again," she said.

"That's what you said the last time."

"But I Won't Ever Again."

Mr. Stacey stopped his car and rolled down the window.

"What's the big idea?" he said, reading the sign.

"I'm selling my little sister," Kate explained. "You can buy her, if you promise to be nice to her."

"Well, I don't know," said Mr. Stacey. "What I really wanted was a nice glass of lemonade."

"We're having a summer sale," said Kate. "She can be yours for only a dollar ninety-nine."

"A dollar ninety-nine! That's too much for such a little *Homo sapiens*. Look, let me give you some advice. People don't want to buy little sisters. When the weather's this hot, what they want is a nice, cool glass of lemonade. Now, for a nice, cool glass of lemonade, I'd gladly pay—oh, say, twenty-five cents. Think about it. I'll be back."

He drove off.

"I'm not a *Homo sapiens*," said Abigail, wrinkling her nose.

"Nuts!" said Kate. "I almost had a sale."

"Phoebe's neck was all sweaty," Abby quickly explained. "Because the weather's *this* hot." She fanned herself with her hand.

"So what happened to her other braid?"

"I don't know, but I'll help you look for it."

Kate glared at her little sister. "AND you ate all the strawberries."

For a long time no one else came by. Kate looked up and down the street. She sighed. "Seems like nobody wants to buy a little sister."

Abby sighed, too. "Let's sell lemonade," she said.

Just then Nonna came out into her yard to water her tomatoes. She saw the sign and walked slowly across the street.

"What are you doing, dear?" she said to Kate.

"I'm selling my little sister, Nonna. You want to buy her?"

Nonna lifted her hands into the air. "Oh, my goodness," she said. "Why do you want to sell your little sister?"

"Because she's a pain," Kate said. "She's always messing with my stuff. Somebody used up all my blue nail polish, and I think I know who."

Abby's eyes got very big. She looked at Nonna, but didn't say anything. Inside her shoes, she wiggled her pretty blue toes.

Nonna smiled. "For me, she's a nice little girl. How much you want?"

Kate thought for a second. "Twenty-five cents?" she said.

"I buy," said Nonna, putting her hand in the pocket of her dress.

"You won't be sorry," Kate said. "Sometimes she can be a lot of fun."

"I'm not sorry," said Nonna.

Kate said, "And I can still play with her sometimes."

But Nonna said, "Oh, no, sweetheart. When you sell something, she's not yours anymore. Here's your twenty-five cents. Give me the little sister."

Abby jumped down from the stand. She gave Nonna her hand and the two of them started crossing the street. Abby was saying something to Nonna, and Nonna was saying, "Sure, honey."

Kate called after them, "If I have a bad dream, can I put my bathrobe on and come over? Usually when I have a nightmare, I go and get in bed with Abby."

But Nonna didn't seem to hear. She went right up the front steps and into her house. Abby stopped on the porch and wiggled her fingers good-bye. Then she went in, too. The door shut.

Kate clutched the quarter in her hand, and jumped up
and down. "Oh boy, oh boy, oh boy!" she cried. "No more
little sister. This is fun!"

She ran upstairs to the room she used to share with her
sister and started carting all Abby's junk out into the hall.
Under their Memory game she found an old valentine from
Abby. It had a picture of a pig snout on it. Also an eye with
long curly lashes, a heart, and a big U.

After Kate had made the room all nice and neat, she knelt by the window and looked out.

The house was quiet except for the sound of her dad, upstairs in his study, typing away at his typewriter. The street was empty.

She wondered what Nonna and Abby were doing. They were probably doing something fun. It wasn't fair!

Kate looked at the man on the quarter as if it were all his fault.

Kate stood on Nonna's porch and put her mouth down by the mail slot.

"You know," she said, "I've decided my little sister's NOT for sale. You can have your money back." She dropped in the quarter and heard it clatter on the floor.

Nonna opened the door. "How come you don't want to sell your little sister?" she asked, stooping over to pick up the money. "You say she's a lot of trouble."

"Um," said Kate. "She laughs at my jokes."

Abby squinted her eyes and laughed so hard right then and there that you could see every tooth in her head.

"Plus I need someone to help me sell lemonade."

"Me!" said Abby, raising both her hands.

"So can you make us some lemonade, Nonna?" asked Kate.

Abby was jumping up and down. "Can I tell her? I want to tell her!"

Nonna nodded.

"We already made it, Kate! I helped. I put the sugar in."

Nonna carried the lemonade in a big plastic pitcher. Abby carried the paper cups. She was very careful not to drop one.

"We'll sell the lemonade," she was saying to Nonna, "and give you lots of money."

Kate was already at the stand, fixing the sign. Now it said,

LITTLE SISTER Brand
LEMONADE FOR SALE.

EDUCATION